Fairytales for Feminists

Attic Press, Dublin.

First published by
Attic Press,
44 East Essex Street,
Dublin 2.

G L
PR 8876.2
r W 65
M 33
1987

Mad and bad fairies: a collection of feminist fairytales.
   1. Short stories, English   2. Feminism — Fiction
   3. English fiction — 20th century
   I. Crone, Joni   II. Kelly, Maeve   III. Dorcey, Mary
   823′.01′0835 [FS]   PN6120.95.F3/

ISBN 0-946211-40-X

Illustrations: Paula Nolan
Cover Design: Paula Nolan
Typesetting: Phototype-Set Ltd., Dublin
Printing: Leinster Leader

An *Irish Fairy Tale* by Frances Molloy
first appeared in *The Female Line: Northern Irish Women Writers*

The publishers wish to thank all of the women who sent in stories, in particular those whose stories were not included due to lack of space.

CONTENTS

The Fate of Aoife
and the Children of Aobh

T HIS is the story of two sisters, their children and the fate brought upon them by the jealousy and dominance of warring men and how one sister, Aoife, transformed that fate.

It is a story that has been told many times but the full truth has not yet been set down.

In the age of the Tuatha de Danaan after the battle of Tailltin there was a rivalry between two Kings; Bodb Dearg and Lir of the Hill of the White Fields whom he had defeated for the Lordship.

Now it happened that Lir's wife died after an illness and Bodb Dearg wanting to placate Lir and win his fealty offered him as a bride Aobh, the eldest of his three foster daughters. And Lir accepted and married her, pleased not only by Aobh's beauty and high birth but by the influence the marriage brought him.

In the course of time a daughter Fionnuala was born to Aobh and later on a son. It was not until many years later, however, when these children were well grown that she conceived again, this time giving birth to twin boys; Fiachra and Conn. But in giving them life she forfeited her own.

All the people of the land keened Aobh. And when Bodb Dearg learnt of it he too mourned her. For he had been proud of Aobh and well satisfied with the loyalty she had won from his son-in-law. So when in due time he was told that Lir was once more looking for a wife, to maintain that friendship he announced that he would make him a gift of another woman; Aobh's younger sister Aoife.

Lir was flattered and more than pleased to find a wife so quickly with so little trouble to himself. He had felt the loss of

Aobh and needed a mother for his four children.

But there was no joy in Aoife's heart when she discovered what they had planned for her: that she was to marry this ageing man who had buried two wives already and the last her own sister. She knew little of him that could not be said of her father and brothers and for all she knew most men; that he was courageous in battle, shrewd in the conduct of his affairs, a proud, possessive man who loved wine and horses above all else. One consideration however, outweighed the rest, one he and her father knew nothing of — when Aobh was dying she had sent for Aoife, the sister with whom she had from the first days of their fosterage a special bond and taking her hand asked her to promise that should she die Aoife would love and protect her four children as if they were her own. And Aoife weeping, had given her promise.

So when Lir came to her father's court with his chariots and retinue she married him and returned to his household.

And it was a strange thing for the young Aoife to live in the house she had known as her sister's guest, to find herself mistress of that household. It was strange and painful to walk in the gardens, eat at the table, sleep in the bed that had been her sister's. Everything she did reminded her of Aobh and increased her sense of loss. But one consolation she had and it was an abundant one: the company of the children, Fionnuala, Aodh, Fiachra and Conn. These four were said to be the most beautiful in Ireland. No one seeing them could resist enchantment. And it was not only beauty they possessed but grace, intelligence and a rare sweetness of nature.

Every hour of the day they played together, the four children and their step-mother and in their lightness of heart and gaiety they were more like five children than four. In the woods and rivers of the White Fields they ran like fawns or wild young horses, in the evening they gathered by the fires of the great hall to tell stories and listen to the music of Aoife's harp.

Lir saw little of them. A lord and warrior, his affairs required much journeying; administering his lands, dealing with his subjects, playing chess with rival chieftains, hunting deer and fishing salmon. But when he was at home he felt the new mood of festivity in the house. And seeing the delight they had in each other's company, his young wife and children, he was torn between excitement and jealousy. Proud beyond sense of their beauty he would snatch up his small sons one in each fist and wave them high in the air, and Fionnuala he would take galloping on horseback holding her before him, her red-gold hair blowing about her to exhibit to all who passed.

One day, saying that with all his travel he was too much deprived of them he ordered the servants to make up their beds in the room next to his. From then on every night before sleeping he would steal in to gaze upon them and in the morning so exuberant and possessive was his affection that immediately upon waking he would go in to their room and lie down with them.

In the spring of that year Aoife found she was with child. As her time drew near she was frightened, being so young and remembering the pain it had cost her sister. Lir, however, was overjoyed for it was the one thing left for him to want; a child of this new union to show the world that he was not yet an old man. But though the birth did not cost Aoife what it had Aobh, the infant was born early and born dead. It was mourned and buried while Lir was away in another Kingdom. When he returned and learnt what had happened he was taken by a fit of rage that put fear in all who saw it. He went straight to Aoife and finding her lying white faced and exhausted it was not pity or tenderness he felt but an increase of anger. He berated her with a ferocity she had not known before. He accused her of carelessness. If she had not insisted on sporting and playing with his children as if she was a child herself, he said, instead of a mother, this blight would not have come upon them. And he went from the room cursing her.

It was bitter beyond knowing for Aoife to be blamed for the death that was her greatest sorrow.

A coldness came between them from that day forward. Lir's journeys became more frequent and prolonged. When he was at home he avoided Aoife and spoke little to her. But though he shunned his wife he was more than ever possessive of his sons and daughters. He would sit late into the night feasting and drinking with his warriors and when at last he rose for sleep it was not to Aoife's room he went but to the children's. He boasted of them hourly and demanded their company at every moment, but a harshness and discontent had entered his affection so that no matter how they studied to please him he was never satisfied.

Aoife saw this and was frightened. She thought it was his anger with her that corrupted his feeling. She saw how he petted and made much of Fionnuala, wooing her praise as if only it could restore his self esteem. But she believed she had no power to influence him, hostile and resentful as he had become to her.

The time arrived when she must make a visit to her foster parents. Not wanting to leave, weary still from the death of the child, she nonetheless made her preparations. Fionnuala came to her, who nearest in age was also closest to her heart. She asked Aoife not to leave her alone with Lir who was so demanding of her. Aoife soothed her and promised a swift return. And setting out she left the children in their father's care.

She was absent from them seven weeks and in that time there was not an hour that she did not think of them. At last, her strength renewed, she departed from Bodb Dearg's kingdom and began her journey to the White Fields. As she drove past Loch Dairbreach she felt a sudden apprehension and she could not persuade the horses to go quickly enough. When she approached the palace there was a strange quiet to it. Lir was away from home, his dogs and horses and servants gone with him. She stood in the courtyard and called for Fionnuala and Aodh but they did not answer. She called the names of Fiachra and Conn and silence remained. She searched the house for them and at length found them quiet together in the furthest room of the house. When she saw the fear in their eyes she was afraid to question them. She stood hesitant on the threshold and they ran to her and threw themselves into her arms weeping. At evening she talked

alone to Fionnuala and discovered what she already feared and what Fionnuala had scarcely words to tell her. Their father had come late from table every night after heavy drinking, laughing and crying at once, lamenting his dead wife and child, had come to the room she shared with her brothers and slept in her bed. And Fionnuala, though hardly more than a child herself, was with child and its father was her own father, Lir of the Hill of the White Fields.

Hearing this, pain went through Aoife's breast like a sword. The children she loved above life, whose protection she had been charged with, she had left uncared for, unguarded. And was it not her fault if this great harm had come to them? But what was she to do? Could she pit herself against Lir? Lir who had a man's power and a King's power and a husband's power. What had she to set against these?

She bade the children to dress and prepare for a journey. She knew if it was to be done she must leave at once before any soul guessed her thought, before she lost courage and resolution for it. Putting a dagger to the left of her cloak and a druid wand to the right of it and taking food enough for three days they set out in one chariot.

They travelled without rest until nightfall. They slept in the forest and woke at first light. Aoife had in the beginning thought of seeking refuge in her father's kingdom, but as they drew near his land she knew it held no sanctuary for her. It was to Lir his loyalty was pledged. He would not believe her story. They would call her an unnatural woman who stole her husband's children out of jealousy.

Later that day they stopped to eat by a river and learnt from some woodmen that Lir of the White Fields was pursuing, with a great troop of horses, the wife who had carried off his children. And Lir's heart, they said, 'was a core of hatred for her and when he found this woman no punishment would be fit for her'.

Terror gripped Aoife and despair at her helplessness. She called the children to her and drove off at once hiding her face so that they would not see the fear. They travelled once more without pause until evening and lay down to sleep in the open, their white and their yellow cloaks spread over them. When the boys slept, Fionnuala spoke to her; 'promise me Aoife', she said, 'that we will never return to the house of Lir'. And Aoife promised her.

The next morning it was not the song of thrush and blackbird that woke them but the shouts of men and the baying of hounds. Hearing them Aoife rose immediately. She thought she might prolong their time if she crossed water and confused the dogs. They were near Loch Dairbhreach, the Lake of the Oaks and it was to there they fled.

The waters of the Loch were wide and dark blue, set in a bracelet of mountains. Seeing the cool, beautiful surface the youngest boys forgot their fear and stopped to bathe. Aoife drove the chariot through shallow water until she emerged further down between two high trees. Fiachra and Conn left off their garments and entered the water and after a moment, seeing their joy, Fionnuala and Aodh followed. They played in the waters then all four, careless and delighting as they had once been in their father's garden. And Aoife watching was the only one to hear the hounds draw near.

Conn the youngest came to the bank and turning eyes upon her clear and green as the fern that grew along the shore he asked:

'We will not go back Aoife, will we? We will stay here free and wild as fish or birds always'.

'Yes', Aoife answered him; fear beating up in her heart so that she could scarcely stand. In a few more minutes Lir would be upon them, they would be parted forever and still she could not fasten her resolve.

Taking Conn's hand she walked into the lake. She cursed herself because she had not the courage to do the only thing she could think of to save them. She stood trembling in the cold water, her hand on his shoulder. Then Fiachra came swimming towards her arching his fine curving neck:

'Look Aoife, what am I now?'

And seeing him she understood and knew what she must do. From under her cloak she took the druid rod and walking close to where they swam she touched with it first the head of

Conn, then Fiachra, then Aodh and then Fionnuala until they were turned, the children, into four swans, white and strong and beautiful.

'It is with flocks of birds your cries will be heard now always', she called triumphantly. And they bent their smooth heads to her outstretched hands.

'You will keep your own voices and sing the sweet music of the Sidhe and your own sense and nobility will stay with you so that it will not weigh too heavy on you to be in the shape of birds', and pushing them gently from her she said sorrowfully:

'Go away out of my sight now, with your white faces and your stammering Irish, children of Aobh'.

And when Lir arrived with his dogs and horses and army he saw his wife standing alone in the rippled water and behind her on the shore the white and yellow cloaks of his children. And he was certain then that she had murdered them.

He dragged her to his chariot and he and all his army set out for her father's kingdom.

And as he rode in fury from the lake he did not see the four white swans that sailed along the shore singing music of such beauty that even the dogs and horses turned to listen. But Aoife heard and gazed back over her shoulder.

At her father's house she was brought before the court. They denounced her with terrible words.

'No punishment was fit', Lir said, 'for a woman who would murder children.' They called her a witch and a demon and the King declared that he would put her into that shape for all time so that no man would look on her face again.

But as the rod fell on her and they cursed her, a witch of the air, Aoife's soul gave thanks. For in that shape though trapped in air she could fly above the power of men to any place on earth her heart desired, far or near.

On the lakes and rivers of Ireland for many hundreds of years, four white swans sailed the clear waters singing music of such sweetness that women and men from all over the land came to hear it and every trouble and sickness they had was quieted by its beauty. And as they moved on the waters, the swans lifted their white heads and gazed into the air as if they beheld something unseen there that gave them protection and delight.

Mary Dorcey

Prologue

In the first chapter Alice had drifted onto Thunderland after setting out from her own country of Harmony Land on a little fishing expedition. Being a very resourceful young person, like everyone else in Harmony Land, she was not unduly worried when she encountered the very strange species of people known as memblys, who were outraged when they discovered that a fem, or female person, could speak for herself and not just out of 'chatter time' as was the rule in Thunderland. She had a narrow escape from the word worshippers who were mumbling praise in front of a totem pole erected to the memory of their word gods. Alice of course escaped from their clutches.

Now read on.

The first chapter of *Alice in Thunderland* appeared in *Ms Muffet and Others,* also published by Attic Press.

Alice in Thunderland

A T the end of her first day in Thunderland Alice felt
exhausted. She had met the strangest creatures
imaginable. Her effort to understand them was
beginning to produce a dangerous lethargy which she had
never before experienced but which she knew from her
training manual had to be resisted.

Her lethargy was in strong contrast to the excitement and
energy she seemed to produce in those whom she met — who
were, of course, all memblys. She had not met one single
fembly. She might have believed they did not exist were it not
for the fact that they were so frequently mentioned in the
memblys' conversations. References were always disparaging,
the mildest being a phrase frequently repeated, 'Oh femblys',
accompanied by a raucous laugh or a peculiar curling of the lip
which she recognised as depicting distaste or contempt.

There were other customs which she was not yet able to
identify and her inability to decode them added to her
weariness. She tried the various reasoning methods she had
been taught in Harmony Land, beginning with 'cool assessment' but the memblys talked so loudly and with such
strength of belief it was impossible to escape their assaults.
Their words had the force of weapons. They seemed to
surround her with their extraordinary logic and she began to
feel not only tired but hemmed in.

It was time for seclusion, she decided. She found a con-
venient nook under a bush and curled herself into a little ball,
turning herself into herself to recharge her interior strength
while resting. She shuteye and deafed ear, so enclosing herself
in her capsule of being that restoration might be quickly
achieved. However, as a wise precaution, so that she might

not be totally unaware, (a dangerous state in this Thunderland), she left on her extra sensory perceptions.

Fifteen minutes later they registered feeling. She woke up, completely refreshed and relaxed and uncurled herself from self to take note of her perceptions. Somewhere in the vicinity something was happening. The vibrations were remarkable. She resumed seeing and hearing and wound her way through a curving path (the first such curve she had come across) to their source.

Two creatures were sitting by a stream, staring into the water. One was definitely a membly, she could tell by the set of the head on the neck and by the shape of its shoulders. They weren't square exactly, but they had a kind of bluntness about them, an assertion of something or other. It didn't matter to Alice what they were asserting. It just struck her as odd that they did. The other creature was definitely not a membly. Alice had met enough of them to be certain. This creature had a different set of head. Her body co-ordination was subtler and more supple. Her voice, when she spoke had something of the timbre of Alice's and it was this voice which had activated her vibrations. There was no doubt in Alice's mind. This creature must be the missing fembly. At long last she was going to meet the female variety. They must be very scarce, Alice thought. She had met sixty three memblys and this was the first fembly. Sixty three to one was long odds. No cat race would be worth an entry in Harmony Land if the odds were so high. They must have a scarcity value. She calculated the odds versus scarcity equation, using the formula for dissimilar forces and the answer was farce. Oh dearie me, thought Alice and then was struck by the voice.

It appeared to be crying.

'I can't stand it anymore', the voice was saying, 'I just can't stand it.'

'You're always saying that,' the membly replied, 'I don't know what's wrong with you. You have everything.'

'I have nothing. Nothing. I am nothing,' the fembly's voice anguished, 'I wish I was dead.'

Alice clapped her hands to her ears. The pain of this remark made her reel.

'Oh forgive, forgive,' she cried in response. 'Forgive. Forgive.' Her pain eased. She rushed towards the couple intending to help the membly restore the life wish to his partner. But to her astonishment he calmly reached for a green bag lying on the grass from which he drew out some wriggling worms. He then attached them to a long line on a stick.

The fembly stood up and moved away from him. The death wish was heavy in her heart. It beat and whined and snarled and moaned. Alice began the forgive chant but nothing could keep the pain from taking over. She rushed out in front of the creature crying, 'stop, stop.'

'What—,' the fembly did stop, amazed. 'What do you want,' she asked angrily.

The death wish faded.

'It gave me a headache,' Alice said. 'Why did you do it?'

'I didn't do anything. What business is it of yours? I was having a private conversation. It is not civil to eavesdrop.'

'A private conversation?' Alice tried to work out what this might be.

'What did Eve drop?' she asked helpfully.

'Very funny, I don't think,' the girl sneered, 'Eve dropped her knickers, of course. It's always the same.'

'Did she lose the knickers?' Alice asked. 'Did she want them badly? Did she miss them? Is that why you made the death wish?'

'You're a crazy person,' the fembly said, backing away.

Alice didn't want her to go. If she couldn't understand this creature who was surely something like herself, judging from the vibrations, how would she ever be able to understand the others. The whole adventure was becoming almost too risky. If she was attacked by any more confusion she might become too weak to make her way back. She did a quick assessment of her remaining resources. With sufficient retreat time for selfconfirmation she should be able to manage. In any case, her virtue of insatiable curiosity had to be nourished and used.

In Harmony Land her gift had produced many useful devices which had given everyone much happiness. Even here, in this danger country she might learn and achieve.

'I felt your death wish,' she said carefully, choosing the words delicately, 'I felt for you.'

With these words the fembly suddenly began to make the most horrible noise Alice had ever heard. Water flowed in torrents from her eyes, spilling down her cheeks and onto the ground. A little rivulet formed at Alice's feet and she felt herself sinking, sinking down. She closed her eyes and concentrated. If it be for good, let me go down. If I learn and achieve let me go down. She felt the earth subside under her and just as she went spinning down down into another territory the fembly clasped her arms around her, still letting the water gush from her eyes, but with the dreadful sound now silenced.

Alice opened her eyes. Much to her relief the fembly had stopped watering but she still clung to Alice.

'My golly,' she said, 'I've heard of this place but I never thought I would find myself in it. How did you manage it? You're a right weirdo. What will the lirgs say when I tell them? They'll never believe it. They certainly won't believe it.' She began to hum to herself, a pleasant little tune which Alice picked up and sang with pleasure.

'What place is it?' she asked, but without waiting for an answer and shaking herself free of the fembly's grip so that she could investigate.

'It's the funnery,' the fembly said. 'The only funnery in the whole of Thunderland. This is where all the laughing and singing and making and doing goes on. The funns were banished years ago because they were too powerful and too optimistic. They were for change and they used to say treasonable things like,' she paused and put her hand to her forehead. 'I've forgotten. I used to know it. My grandmother taught me a few of the lines but they were all wiped out by re-learning and of course by ignoring. Ignoring and silence are very important parts of femblys' education.'

Alice was sure she had picked up a dodo. A dumdum. This

creature was even worse than the memblys. She glanced cautiously at her to see if her brains were showing.

'Have you brains?' Alice asked politely.

The fembly became very agitated.

'You mustn't say that. Someone might hear. Oh, I forgot. It's safe here. I used to have more brains but some of them turned into feathers. Look.'

Sure enough a little tuft of feathers showed through her hair.

'How did you get those?' Alice asked with interest.

'It took a long time. I had to read the prescribed texts and never ask the questions I wanted to ask. I had to learn not to do the things I thought were useful, or to think the things I thought were important. That was very hard. I had to stifle imagination and turn down feeling. Femblys' feelings are too strong, you know. Every now and again they take over and they gush out in torrents. That's what happened a while ago.'

'Well,' Alice said. 'Then it was your feelings that brought us here. It's a good trick. I must learn it. It's practically an achievement,' she added kindly, not wishing to sound begrudging.

'I remember, I remember,' the fembly cried aloud. 'I remember grandmother's saying. Beware of the dirty tricks brigade. Always look a gift house twenty times. Never sign on the dotted line. Never say I do. Always ask why. Worry about a persecution complex when the persecutor is dead. Grow a wisteria for the doctor's hysteria. A woman wears an apron to cook a banquet. A man wears a crown to boil a haddock.'

She would have continued on but Alice's attention had been taken by a great construction looming out of the dark undergrowth in front of them. It was like an enormous yellow drum. On its round face a huge sunflower was painted and Alice then noticed that the sides of the clearing where they had landed were lined with sunflowers apparently growing upside down. Their stalks trailed upwards towards the earth, their heads rested on the ground below them, releasing a gentle, yellow light.

The centre of the sunflower on the building was a huge smiling face. The petals consisted of a circle of arms waving and gesticulating. As Alice and the fembly approached, the face spoke. It sounded like chiming bells.

'Welcomy, welcomy. Come in well and truly dearest friends. Open your hearts and your minds, my treasures, my pets. My doty ones. Oh pulse of my hearts and brightness of brightness. Enter the place of happiness. Pray be seated if you will, or pray stand if you will not. Happily you may remember and happily you may forget. Whatever is mine is yours, whatever is yours is anyone's. Please enter on the sixth note. Thanking you, signing off, your best friend and delight of your life, my love, my dove, my beautiful one. Afem.'

Alice was busily engaged in translating this effusive welcome when the sixth bell chimed, the mouth which had been uttering the words turned into an elaborate doorway, a silver coloured drawbridge was lowered and two beautiful, longhaired, silver eyed, pink furred cats stepped out of the sunflower, curtseying as they came to Alice and the fembly.

'Your pleasure is our pleasure,' they sang in unison, perfectly in tune. 'Follow us to the gathering of funns. You are just in time to hear the first debate. We have been awaiting you.'

'Oh. I feel sick,' the fembly groaned.

'Breathe deeply, count to ten, think of your grandmother,' Alice instructed.

They followed the pink cats along the silver roadway through the sunflower doormouth and into the most splendid of palaces. As they entered they had to duck all the waving petal arms whose hands were catching at Alice's hair, the fingers getting entangled and pulling tufts of it out. Alice was not too pleased at this. She frowned a little.

Instantly a great bell boomed throughout the building. Lights flashed purple, yellow, orange, green, blue, spotted, striped in an incredible combination of colours. The cats leaped and hissed and stared at Alice, arching their backs, their silvery eyes gleaming.

The fembly clung to Alice's arm. In front of them, great

purple velvet curtains swished to one side revealing rows of creatures with their heads turned and their hundreds of laughing eyes directed straight at Alice. One of them stood up. She was about Alice's own height. Her hair was silky and striped with pink and yellow bars. It hung over her shoulders. She was wearing coloured balloons. As she moved they continually burst and she continually laughed, blew up another and attached it wherever she pleased.

'You frowned,' she said sweetly. 'You set our alarms off. Did you have a bad thought, you naughty thing.'

Alice was surprised to find herself amused by this question and not in the least wearied because she did not understand it. The creature was so merry and the colours so enchanting she felt a cloudy haze envelop her thought. Just in time she switched on her protection from exaggerated impulses and the cloud shifted.

The creature who had addressed her appeared to be the head of the funnery. She twiddled her fingers and all the funns rose up and sang Pale, poley, pean, pother of Percy, pale. They burst out laughing, leaped out of their seats and began to dance extravagantly, throwing their legs and arms around, shaking their heads, while the room filled with the sound of music from hundreds of instruments.

The fembly was overcome with joy and rushed to join them, singing in a strange high voice in an unfamiliar language. Alice began to laugh and the more she laughed the louder grew the singing. Her head began to swim with the noise. Her own laughter made her sick.

'Stop,' she cried, 'you foolish creatures. Show me what you can make or do.'

As if she had turned a switch, everything stopped. At a signal from the head funn, all the funns filed past her towards another room. The fembly was lost in the crowd. She seemed to have been swallowed up. Alice followed the crowd whose previously rainbow coloured clothes and hair was being changed before her eyes into peculiar dark grey coloured body and leg covers. They wore white tops under these grey coverings and around their necks were dark strips of cloth, hidden under the collars, but appearing as a narrow line on the tops. Alice wondered if they could be choked by these ties, if the blood supply to their brains might not be impeded, but she was interested in seeing how these, the first of the femblys she had met in memblyland occupied their time usefully. It would surely be better than the word worshipping memblys she had met earlier and whom she had been obliged to whip into line when they tried to take advantage of her.

She was last to enter the next room, apart from the two pink cats who trailed behind her, obviously keeping their silver eyes on her. All the funns were seated in rows of benches and had already begun working on an enormous, intricately worked lace cloth. It seemed to Alice that there were acres and acres of this beautiful material. The funns had their heads bent and their nimble fingers moved quickly through the delicate patterns. The head funn sat at a table and held up a picture of a bearded membly who had a sun-flower over his head, but was unmistakably a membly nonetheless.

'Remember,' the head funn said, 'My sisters, my dears. Your work is for the good of your soles so that your feet may dance nimbly and will do honour at the same time to our dear Rescuer. Let us give thanks. Let us play. But not just yet.'

The fembly had joined Alice at the doorway. Alice was delighted to see her familiar face.

'What are they making?' she asked, 'and who is the Rescuer?'

'The Rescuer is the chief of all time and place and space and everything and nothing. The funns make trimmings for the memblys who guard his presence.'

'But I thought you said the memblys had banished the femblys,' Alice asked feeling confused, 'And isn't the Rescuer a membly? And couldn't the funns make a sail instead of this trimming so that they could get away from this terrible place?'

'It's not a terrible place,' the fembly said. 'It's full of love and sunshine.'

'They're only sunflowers,' Alice said. 'It's all artificial. I don't think much of it. I prefer proper sunshine. And when is the debate?'

'I'm going to water again,' the fembly gasped. 'You're ruining everything. I can feel a watering coming on.'

'I'll get you a bucket,' Alice said helpfully. But it was too late. The fembly had already begun. Waterfalls spilled from her eyes. In seconds the ground was a marsh. In minutes it was a lake. All the benches were turned upside down and the funns sat in them, paddling merrily with their hands. The head funn called out,

'In this time of crisis, let us begin our great debate.' Alice managed to procure a small table for herself and pulled the fembly and the pink cats up to share it with her.

'I'd like to join in,' she called.

But the head funn had paddled away rapidly from her, shouting 'Haven't you done enough damage? Go back where you came from. We can do without your sort here. Blow-in. Runner.'

Alice sighed heavily. They had gone through the now soggy velvet curtains and were being swept along towards the sunflowermouth exit. What would await them outside? She was filled with even more insatiable curiosity. There were more adventures waiting.

*   *   *   *   *

What will happen Alice? Will she be able to get out of the funnery? Where did the word worshippers go? Will she meet more memblys? Will she ever get back to Harmony Land?

Read all about it in the next instalment.

Maeve Kelly

Ophelia's Tale

(Ophelia is on the phone to her friend Simone).

DOGGONE it Simone, how was I to know it would turn out like this? The royals didn't make it easy either, at least not in the beginnin', or even in the end, come to think of it. I never felt at home in that spooky castle anyway. Bein' run out of New Orleans was tough on Papa, Polonius to you, or Old Baloney as his friends back then called him. But endin' up in a damp old castle in Denmark is goin' too far if you ask me. Larry, that's the kid brother Laertes, didn't mind it as much as I did, but then he was always Papa's favourite and he got in with a wild bunch anyway and had a rare old time of it.

If Mama was alive of course none of this would have happened in the first place. She was too strong and stubborn to let a little bad luck force her into grovellin' to anyone, even Kings, unlike Old Baloney.

I tell you Simone, Papa was so upset the day he was washed ashore here, when the old king, the one Claudius knocked off, thought we was pirates. He said his blood was stirred. I didn't understand why he was so upset but then old Papa is the vain sort — Mama always said so. Well, from that day to this he made a special effort to prove that we was people of consequence. He became a right old lickboots if you ask me. And Larry isn't much better at times.

It's gettin' right bad since the murder. Don't get me wrong now, I do really love Papa but I must have been right crazy to agree to Papa's plan, (pause) to pretend to love that looney Hamlet. I mean you can see my point of view can't you, Simone? Who wants to love a prince that does nothin' all day, 'cept read old creepy books. Then at night when we're up on

the battlements he starts a talkin' to his dead daddy jes like his daddy's still alive.

The plan! I'm comin' to the plan Simone, jes be patient. Yer gettin' to be just like all the rest, rushin' an' fussin.' I mean I feel bad now that Claudius has turned out to be a regular asshole. Hamlet and myself nearly went nuts last month with those creeps Rosencrantz and Guildenstern followin' us everywhere on Claudius's orders. It got so bad I had to look in the bathroom before I'd use it.

The play was the worst. Claudius was screamin', Gertrude was cryin' and Hamlet was laughin', and the worst of all was when poor Papa was run through 'cos Hamlet says he thought he was a rat. I mean you'd want to be nuts to believe a story like that.

I'm goin' to get even with him for that, I swear it. Remember that magic shop in town, the one we visited last spring. Well, I went in there yesterday and I bought that colourless dinghy — the trick one — that makes it seem like you're floatin' on water. (pause) I know it's tricky Simone but to be quite honest I just don't care anymore. Even if it doesn't work an' I do drown at least when Hamlet gets back from England he'll have a real corpse to view. Maybe then he'll stop seein' his dead daddy everywhere. (pause) Oh don't be like that Simone! Don't be sorry! Sure I'll miss you too but another winter in this damp old dump with lunatics would really drive me nuts. (pause) There's a knock on my door Simone. Got to go. I bet it's Claudius askin' me to do more flower arrangin'.

One way or another, I'm glad I'm goin', Simone.'

Clairr O'Connor

Thumbelina the Left Wing Fairy

NCE upon a time in the Land of Nod lived a tiny little girl called Thumbelina. No one shook hands or said 'hello' in this land, instead everyone nodded and winked all the time because a nod was as good as a wink, although nods were used for strangers and winks for people you knew well and liked.

People slept a lot of the time in the Land of Nod because no one wanted to make a sound. People who lived by the sea didn't want to rock the boat because that would make waves. You could hear a pin drop any hour of the day and when it did everyone scurried in fear of the Giant. To these little thumb-size creatures when the penny dropped it sounded as if someone had dropped a clanger. It dropped once a year when the giant was counting his money. He had so much piled on his table he couldn't budge it. It glistened and gleamed but the Giant couldn't count it because he had sticky fingers. With the money that stuck to his fingers he played push ha'penny with himself. But this Giant was very stupid. He didn't know that one and one makes two so, since he made the rules he decided that the first goal scored won the game. He spent a lot of time tabling motions until he finally scored. That was when the penny slid off the table and dropped into the grass.

Down in the grass roots lived the little people. The Giant was big and strong and lived very far removed from the grass roots. His name was Jargon but his friends called him Cliche. He got where he was by having a Party and walking all over everyone. Every year the Balloons in his Party caused Inflation and the little people were fed up with all the hot air. Nevertheless they ran to the tree and waited for crumbs from the rich man's table. When the penny dropped they turned it into a

table and sat around the table and made laws. These were called the Tables of the Law. To finish this annual general meeting everyone cried 'Holy Moses', but no one knew why.

Little Thumbelina slept most of her life. The penny dropped when she was born. People used to give her the thumbs up on the rare occasions when she left her bed and the rest of the time they talked about her as the Gifted Dreamer. Then one day she woke up.

She climbed the tree to the top until she held the floor. Then she took the chair and climbed and climbed until she tabled a motion and found herself at the top of the heap. The Giant stirred in his sleep. The money was all piled up on the Right. She pushed the money to the Left until it came raining down into the grass roots and all the little people woke up. Now everyone had a table and each individual could make their own laws to suit themselves.

Ever since then people in the Land of Nod have lived by rule of thumb and no one has been any the wiser.

Joni Crone

Some day my prince will come

Some day my prince will come
And carry me away
But my social life's so hectic
I just hope I'm in that day.
Roisin Sheerin

The Frog Prince

ONCE upon a time, in a far off land, there lived a King and Queen with three beautiful daughters. The eldest, the auburn-haired Princess Marigold, decided, at the age of 18, that life at court was not for her and one night she slipped out of the Palace, leaving a note on the hall table, and got the boat to England. Having signed on for the dole, she was now travelling round the country with a well-known pop star. She was in other words a groupie. The Palace Press Officer explained her absence by saying that she was following a musical career abroad and, in a way, that's just what she was doing.

The second daughter, the blonde Princess Esmerelda, had also opted out and become involved with a strange religious sect. She was to be seen in the main shopping street of the capital stopping passers by and trying to convert them. Luckily, she used an assumed name and, with her head shaved, except for a long pony tail, strange painted marks on her nose and a long blue robe, she was quite unrecognisable. The statement from the Palace announced that Her Royal Highness had taken up missionary work.

The raven-haired Princess Matilda was the youngest daughter and she was by far the fairest, if you know what I mean. By the time she had come of age, the Kingdom was in such a sorry state that the King had been forced to borrow enormous sums of money and now he was out of his tiny mind trying to think of ways to meet the interest payments. He was also worried that his subjects might begin to ask awkward questions if he allowed another daughter to fade into obscurity. After all, they had to have someone as a leader of fashion, didn't they?

Then, as the King sat in his jacuzzi one morning, a smile came over his face. Inspiration had hit him at last. He would marry Matilda off, just like they used to in the golden days. She'd object naturally at first, but she was a kind young woman and fond of her old Dad. He thought he could talk her round — the promise of a crown jewel or two might help. They were only paste but would she know? He closed his eyes and thought with pleasure of all the revenue a Royal wedding would bring — TV and film rights, video sales, seats on the processional route, souvenirs, special issues of stamps and how about an increase in tax on flags and bunting? Just think of all the tourists who would come flooding into the country and, another thing, a distraction like this might get the workers off his back for a bit.

But who could he persuade to marry her and, more important, who could she be persuaded to marry? Princess Matilda was certainly attractive but unfortunately at her Christening the 'Wicked' Fairy had wished brains on her, a fate which hadn't befallen the Princes in the neighbouring lands. Most of the good-looking Princes were either working as male models (not quite the image he was looking for in a son-in-law) or were busy trying to get into television. One, Prince Richard, had succeeded and was now to be seen reading the News — incognito, of course.

No, he'd have to look farther afield. Hold on, what about Prince Phillippe of France — no danger of his becoming a male model and his family had money and might be willing to go halves with the wedding expenses.

Prince Phillippe was not a pretty sight, well below average height (a spiteful person might have described him as a dwarf) and beginning to run to fat. He already had a slight stoop and his extreme bow-leggedness gave him a most unusual walk. His large protruding eyes were a rather unpleasant muddy colour and his croaky voice and thick accent made him very hard to understand.

Try as he might, the King couldn't think of another candidate, so he approached Prince Phillippe's family to sound them out. Naturally, they were delighted with the suggestion. They had long ago given up hope of finding anyone shortsighted enough to want to marry their son. So eager were they, that they offered to pay threequarters of the wedding costs if necessary. Prince Phillippe seemed pleased as well.

'So far, so good,' said the King to himself, 'now to persuade Matilda to marry Phillippe.'

'I hadn't really planned on getting married at all, Papa,' she began when he put his proposition to her. So he quickly brought up the subject of the crown jewels, hoping to tempt her, but Matilda was not to be won over with the promise of jewels.

'Oh, come off it, Papa,' she laughed. 'As a child, I always suspected they were paste, so I did a chemical analysis on them to make sure.'

'Oh, those wretched brains of hers.' The King sighed and then realised his daughter was still speaking.

'Anyhow, that sort of stuff is considered pretty hick nowadays. I mean, how many people wear tiaras to discos?'

The King scratched his head, that was a poser and no mistake. 'I give up,' he said at last.

'Oh, Papa, you really are a fool,' Matilda said, affectionately squeezing his arm.

'Thank you, my dear,' he said, trying to look suitably modest.

'Look, Papa, I can see the mess you're in and I'd like to help. I feel rather sorry for this poor Phillippe person, I mean he looks so grotty but I'll agree to marry him on one condition.'

'Anything, my love!' said the King eagerly.

'That you let me enrol for an evening degree course in Science.'

The King was delighted and readily agreed. Prince Phillippe had no objections to his bride being busy four nights a week. After all, it would leave him free to follow local tradition and spend his evenings in the pub with the other husbands.

The wedding was arranged for September so that the Princess could be back from the honeymoon in time for the start of the academic year.

I won't bore you with all the details of the wedding — weddings are much the same the world over. I will just tell you that Princess Matilda looked beautiful and that the sun shone.

Thanks to Prince Phillippe's family's contribution, there was plenty to eat and drink and then, after a decent interval, the happy couple retired to the Bridal Suite as happy couples are wont to do.

The next morning, at 8 o'clock, there was a tap on the door of the Royal Bedchamber and in came a Palace maid-servant with the early morning tea. She was more than surprised to find Princess Matilda alone.

'Er, excuse me, your Royal Highness,' the maid-servant began, putting the tray down on the bedside table, 'but . . . .'

'Oh, it's quite all right, don't look so worried. His Highness is in the bath. Come and see,' she said, and jumping out of bed, she took the startled girl's hand and pulled her, protesting, into the bathroom. And there in the bath was the most beautiful frog you have ever seen.

'Isn't it wonderful?' Princess Matilda looked radiant. 'You see Zoology is my subject and I'm planning to write a paper on Animal Behaviour and now I have my very own frog. I wonder if a frog could be trained to retrieve balls from wells?' she mused to herself.

Then she smiled dreamily, knowing that she at least was going to live happily ever after.

Anne Cooper

The Witch-hunt

INSIDE her small, sparsely furnished cottage, Minnie Power was making preparations for her evening visitors. A turf fire burned brightly in the wide, open hearth. Leaping tongues of flames licked the bottom of a huge threelegged cauldron which hung from an iron crane in the fire's recess. Minnie's large, black cat, Psyche, relaxed contentedly in an armchair near the hob.

Darkness was closing in and the dancing light from the fire threw shadows and strange shapes on the walls and ceiling. In the centre of the room stood a long wood table covered with bottles of every size, shape and hue; some full, some empty, and all labelled. Books on plants, herbs, spices, medicines and the anatomy of the human body occupied a large bookcase against one wall. Over all hung a delicate fragrance of herbs and spices.

As she busied herself stirring the cauldron with a longhandled enamel spoon and filling the bottles with her lotions and potions, Minnie crooned softly while Psyche purred loudly. Occasionally she consulted a book which lay open on the table.

Minnie was reputed to be a witch. Her one and only companion was Psyche, of whom it was said that at night she turned into a she devil and was really her sister. She did nothing to dispel these rumours, rather she reinforced them by her eccentric dress and, at times, odd behaviour.

Mystery surrounded her past. No one knew exactly where she had come from so there was much speculation about her background. Some said she had been a wealthy woman who had suffered a sad misfortune and was now forced to live in reduced circumstances. Others said she was the daughter of a bishop who had her banished from his sight or that she was an ex-nun discharged for unsubservient behaviour. Nobody ever said 'hello' to Minnie. As she passed by, people would cross themselves and mutter, 'the Lord between us and all harm.'

Although publicly Minnie was ostracised, privately she was much sought after. Over the years she had earned a reputation for being able to cure certain ailments and was particularly wise in matters affecting women's health and wellbeing. At first, no one was ever seen paying her a visit but as her curative powers became better known more and more women called for advice. It was at this juncture that Minnie's problems really began.

The first client to arrive, on this particular day, was Julia Mac who was married to Johnny, the blacksmith. She looked hot and flustered so Minnie offered her a cup of camomile tea.

'Take it easy, Julia. you know what I told you about the blood pressure. Sit down and relax.'

'Thanks Minnie, the drop of scald is very welcome but I haven't come about myself. It's about you. I felt I had to warn you, you've been so good to me in the past. You're the talk of the town and you were read from the pulpit on Sunday. Holy God, but it's a fright, so it is.'

It was probably only a coincidence, but at the mention of the deity, Psyche stretched her legs and bared her claws. Minnie lifted her off the chair and sat down with her on her lap. She whispered a soothing word in her ear.

'I'm used to talk, Julia. You have to develop a thick skin in my line of business. Anyway, when they are talking about me they are leaving others alone.'

'But that's where you are wrong,' said Julia, shaking her head. 'It's not just talk and they're not leaving others alone either. They're saying that you are performing fertility rites in the woods at night, getting couples to leap through blazing bonfires and that you sent Peg Mannion to the city for an unmentionable operation. It's all the fault of them apothecaries and specialists who believe you are queering their pitch. They see you as a threat to their interests. And that's not the holy all of it either. Take a look at what was

given out at the church last Sunday.'

Julia produced a leaflet and thrust it into Minnie's hand. As she read it her expression grew very sad.

BEWARE! SATAN IS AT WORK!

It has come to the notice of concerned citizens of this town that Satan is in our midst in the form of a WITCH. Certain unnatural practices are taking place in the home of Minnie Power which are a threat to our Christian society. All right minded people are called upon to gather outside the
Witch Power's Cottage
at sundown on Wednesday.
Lend a hand in driving Satan from our town.
Organised by
CITIZENS UNITED against PAGAN SORCERY (CUPS)

Julia could see that Minnie was very distressed. 'You'll have to leave, Minnie. It isn't safe for you to stay here any more.'

For a moment Minnie said nothing. Then she stood up straight and tossed her head defiantly, crumpled the leaflet and threw it into the fire. It roared up the chimney in a ball of flame.

'I have no intentions of running away, Julia, because I have done nothing wrong. I will stand my ground and trust in the women whom I have helped over the years. They will explain how I listened to their problems which the professionals wouldn't even admit existed, how I provided them with alternative medicines when others only patronised them, telling them to go home and pull themselves together or else doped them with drugs. They will tell how I comforted and counselled.'

'That highminded talk is all very well, if you don't mind me saying so,' said Julia, 'but I've spoken to some of the women and not all of them are brave enough to stand up and be counted. Don't you see they don't have your independent mind and attitude? You must go into hiding and when it's safe you can make your whereabouts known to us somehow. Don't let the CUPS get you — we need you, Minnie.'

'Thank you, Julia, for your kindness and solidarity but the

time has now come to face the mindless mob. I have been hounded now for too many years. Besides, you will be surprised at the support I will get.'

Julia was disappointed that Minnie wouldn't take her advice. 'I hope you won't regret it. The fanatics in CUPS will stop at nothing to achieve their ends, wait till you see. But you can count on me no matter what.'

On the evening of the demonstration, people began to arrive just before dusk carrying an effigy of Minnie hanging from a pole. They became rowdy, chanting 'We want the Witch' and throwing stones at the windows. Then they made a huge circle and set fire to the effigy. All the while, Minnie sat at the fire stroking Psyche. Every time a window pane broke she let out a caterwaul which excited the mob even more.

In the middle of the commotion the police arrived and through a loudhailer they ordered Minnie to come to the door. When she did the crowd went wild. She was then formally charged with performing unlawful acts of witchcraft and with being the cause of the riot. She was then marched off to the marketplace where she was clamped in the pillory for the night. At the inquisition to be held next day, she would be further charged with bewitching the women of the town, dealing in incantations, charms and spells, encouraging women to visit other witches in the city, concocting love potions and telling fortunes.

Meanwhile, Psyche had made good her escape and was down in the woods frightened out of her wits. Her pitiful screams were soon heard by the local fairy sluagh who emerged from their rath to investigate. Fairies and animals have no difficulty in communicating with each other so in no time at all the fairies had the whole story.

Some of the more undisciplined fairies suggested a blast from the Evil Eye was the only way to break the CUPS and lessen their power but they were overruled and it was finally decided to rescue Minnie from the pillory and take her into safe keeping. Psyche, who was very streetwise, led a procession into the town while the mortals slept. When they reached the pillory poor Minnie was unconscious and looked very much the worse for her experience. She was so well secured with huge iron locks that, try as they would, they were unable to free her.

Then Psyche had an idea. 'I'll go for Johnny the Blacksmith, who is married to Julia Mac. He will pick the locks without any bother and Julia will be a comfort to Minnie.'

The head fairy thought this was mighty. 'We will bestow on you the magic power to turn yourself into a mortal when you reach the forge because Johnny would have a heart attack if he heard a cat talk.'

When Johnny heard the rescue plan he gathered together some tools while Julia yoked the horse and cart. In no time at all they were back at the pillory where Minnie was being kept warm by the fairies and quicker than you could say, 'Women of the World Unite, You've nothing to lose but your Pillories,' Minnie Power was free.

Minnie has been underground ever since but with the help of Psyche and the fairies she is continuing to keep in contact with the women of the town. Her work carries a great deal of danger because the CUPS are still determined to discredit her and banish her for ever.

Máirín Johnston

The Story of Emer

THERE was once in Eireann a woman of courage and tenacity, clearsighted, surefooted and proud. Her name was Emer. She was also known as Omra because of her knowledge of the Ogham stones and Celtic alphabet which she had learned from the Druid priestess Cathbad.

Emer was renowned for her wit. Every man in the Red Branch Knights was cowed by her tongue, for none could match her in repartee, and she was not above bawdiness or profanity, but only when it was called for.

'Each to his measure' she would say, with a wink to the womenfolk.

Now Emer had a sister, Aoife, who was with child and Cathbad the Druid had prophesied that Aoife's first born would bring ruin on Ulster.

'Her child is destined to rule Ulster for a year and a day' said Cathbad, 'and for nine generations thereafter the rivers will run red with the blood of the sons of Usnach'. This curse could be lifted if Aoife fulfilled three conditions:

if she gave birth in a field in the midst of a stone circle
if the afterbirth was buried beneath an Ogham stone and
if she suckled her newborn on the night of the full moon before Samhain.

So it fell to Emer to journey north to Emain Macha for Aoife had been abed a threequarter moon and would surely give birth before the next moon was full. It was seven day's journey from Luachra in the south, past the hill of Tara, across the plains of Meath to Emain Macha.

On waking that morning Emer felt a chill. The first cold wind of autumn was blowing, heralding the winter. But the sky was clear and almost cloudless as she grasped the reins of her horse, a dappled grey mare, and heaved herself into the saddle. She sealed the dark green tweed of her outer garments, drew her purple cloak round her and fastened the silver torc.

Before she set out Cathbad made a further prophecy by giving her three geasa, or prohibitions: she must not rest or descend from her horse in a mist, she must not refuse a game of chess and she must not marry any man living before Samhain, the Celtic new year. If she broke the first two geasa the prophecy would come true, if she broke the third, she herself would die the morning after.

So it was with a light and a heavy heart that Emer set out that day. Her light heart looked forward to the birth of her sister's child, her heavy heart feared the ominous prophecy.

Aisling, her young foster sister accompanied her. Though of slight build and pale complexion, she carried a world of psychic wisdom between her ears. Emer's practical nature made her a little uneasy in the company of Aisling, the girl was so unpredictable and given to fainting fits and crying out in her sleep. But Aisling admired Emer greatly and laughed at her witty remarks so things went well enough the first day. On the second day Aisling looked very pale and troubled, but Emer knew not to pester her with questions so they rode on in silence.

That night Aisling kept muttering the word 'currach' or 'Cormac' and shouting out warnings and omens so that Emer hardly got a wink of sleep all night. Aisling was dreaming about Cormac.

Now Cormac, son of Cliona the brave, was king of Connaught and he had an interest in stopping Emer ever getting to Emain Macha. He had sailed far and wide in his youth, across the Celtic Sea to places with strange sounding names, up the river Sequana to Parisiorum and once, with his mother, he'd gone the full length of the Danubia river. As a man he had journeyed further south and met tribes who showed less respect for their women than did his own Celtic clans. These Romans, as they were called, held all male assemblies and courts. It was Cormac's ambition to see himself at the head of just such a court in Eireann. He began to worship Luga the sun god and paid little attention to the supplications of the druids to the supreme goddess Eire. Nevertheless he could not ignore the power of the Druid priestesses.

Now there was a certain priestess, Fedelma, who was bound by an oath of her grandmother's to grant one wish to Cliona the brave, and one wish to her first born son. Cormac made use of this magic power he had inherited by engaging Fedelma as sorceress to bring about the ruin of Ulster and so make himself High King of all Eire.

Fedelma caused a fog to surround Emer and Aisling so they could not see the ground from the sky. Their pace slowed but they seemed to be still on the path. Unknown to themselves they were heading west instead of east.

With the slow plodding pace Emer's thighs began to ache, her back became as stiff as a rod of iron and a searing pain pierced her neck and shoulders. Her hands clenched the reins in a rigid clamp, her feet had grown numb. Still she was determined not to break the geasa, she did not rest nor descend from her horse.

It wasn't until they reached the Fairy Hill at Cruachan that Aisling knew they had gone astray. She began to chant, then hum, in an odd half musical way. A strange haunting sound it was. Emer was a strong, fearless woman but the sound made her hair stand on end and her teeth chatter. She endured it until she could bear it no longer and pleaded with Aisling to stop.

'I must summon the Sidh,' Aisling answered, 'or we'll be wandering in this mist forever.' The Sidh were the spirits who lived inside the Fairy Hill. At that, a strange birdlike voice spoke from somewhere above their heads.

'I'm the Gatekeeper. You can go no further. Tell me your business and I'll direct you.'

'We've lost our way in the fog. We have to get to Emain Macha,' said Emer impatiently.

'That's no fog but a druidic mist and someone is at pains to stop you getting there,' said the birdlike voice.

'Will you help us?' Aisling asked as though she were talking to a person.

Emer heard a flutter of wings and saw a large black raven

landing on Aisling's shoulder. She watched as the bird plucked something from under its feathers.

'Here, take this,' the squawky voice said.

'What is it?' Emer asked nervously.

'A stone like any other but place it in your palm at moonlight and you'll have a clear path'. The raven's squawk began to sound more human.

'Thank you,' said Emer, 'but who am I indebted to?'

'I am Cliona the Brave,' said the bird. 'A druid put a curse on me the night I died. I must spend three more lifetimes as a raven before I take human form again. Ask me no more now but go on your way'.

The raven flapped its sleek black wings and flew off into the stillness. Emer and Aisling urged their horses on. They had barely taken three more steps when the fog lifted and the plains of Meath spread out before them like a quilt. Emer was sorely in need of a rest but she didn't want to risk any more enchantment and insisted they ride on.

As they reached the shores of Lough Uachter a lone rider came towards them. A handsome young warrior by the look of it, with the scarlet tunic of the Red Branch Knights. In one hand he carried a five pointed spear, in the other a shield embossed with gold. This was a nobleman indeed, thought Emer, though she found it strange that she had been in Emain Macha many times but had never seen this youth before.

'Is it that my sister is delivered of her child before her time?' she asked.

'I know not of that.'

'But you have come from Emain Macha surely?'

'Not I. For I have been travelling a year and a day and it is Omra I seek.'

'Why have you sought me these many days?'

'The wish to play ficheall with you.'

At this Aisling laughed, not knowing of Emer's geasa. 'What sort of ignoramus are you?' she jeered him. 'Don't you know that Emer here has never lost a game of chess in her life and she only plays for the highest stakes?'

'I do,' he said, 'but I am Feargeal Dearg, a champion player

among my own people. And I will wager fifty grey horses, the like of your dappled grey mare, strong, swift, fierce but yokable and fifty jewelled bridles to go with them, if you will play one game with me.'

'I will,' said Emer, 'but you must travel with us to Emain Macha, for no chess set do I carry with me.'

'No need,' he said, 'for a fine set I have here'. True it was, for the board was gilded with bronze, a fish with a half-moon shaped gold spot between the eyes was inlaid on the casing, the pieces were of gold. They set up the board but just as Emer was about to make her first move, Cormac of Connaught appeared before them, with three hundred warriors on either side of him.

'Omra, give me your blessing,' whispered Feargeal.

Emer made the Ogham sign over his weapons, touched his forehead with her thumb and placed her hand on the crown of his head.

'I will best you,' said Feargeal to Cormac, 'if you'll not let us pass.'

'And where's your army?' said Cormac.

'I have the might of the Sidh with me,' answered Feargeal.

'I see no mighty forces here,' said Cormac.

'If I will it, not one man here will live,' said Emer calmly, 'let us pass.'

'I will not,' said Cormac, 'take the long road and no harm will come to you.'

'Do you refuse to move?' said Emer.

'I do,' said Cormac.

'So be it.'

With that Feargeal made the hero's salmon leap down into the middle of the throng. He raised his magic shield and sent it whirling over their heads. The spears bent inwards as the shield hit and in the rushing forward, three hundred were slain by the point of their own spears. When the remaining hordes saw what had happened they turned and fled. And the place has been called Spear Point Hill from that day to this.

Emer and Feargeal returned to their chess playing. Aisling watched for a while, admiring the skill of Feargeal, for indeed he knew the game well, but soon she lost interest and fell asleep, feeling sorry for the handsome warrior who would surely lose.

At dawn, Feargeal departed. Emer did not hold him strictly to his wager, she gave him till Samhain the following year to gather the fifty grey mares he had promised. But lo, at noon, as they were rounding a hill, there stood Feargeal once more with the fifty grey mares grazing in the valley below.

'True to his word,' said Aisling.

'I defend my honour in word and deed,' said Feargeal.

'You speak truly,' said Emer, 'and I thank you for the best game I've played in many a long year. No one showed such skill since Findige, the cousin of my youth. She has since disappeared from my life, but not from my memory. I thank you for the memory also. Now I'll bid you farewell.'

The women rode on northwards till the moon rose. They camped by a river and mused at the shapes the shadows made in the silver light. Aisling looked up at the far hill and saw the unmistakable silhouette of Feargeal Dearg on horseback. But when Emer looked he was gone. 'We'll meet him again,' said Aisling and went to sleep with a look of contentment on her face.

Sure enough, the next day, there was Feargeal at sunset with a bundle of firewood already gathered, inviting them to share his resting place, a fine spot, sheltered from the wind. Again he produced his chess set. This time the wager was the hand of Emer in marriage. Aisling marvelled at his audacity, for Emer was known to shun all suitors, preferring a good storyteller for company or a good game of chess, to all their deeds of valour.

'And what will you wager in return?'

'A further fifty grey mares and add to that fifty red eared cows and fifty storytellers and fifty chess players with skill to match your own.' Emer threw back her head and laughed. This indeed was a wager worth playing for, but even this did not turn her head.

'Take care,' cautioned Aisling, 'for this is a man (if man he is and not a godly spirit) with great power and cunning. You must set him a hard task.' 'And so I will,' whispered Emer gleefully.

'I will take your wager,' said Emer, 'but you must win not one, but two games in succession.'

Feargeal never batted an eyelash but agreed on the spot.

For three days and three nights they played, never stopping for meat or drink or sleep, such was their stamina. In the end Aisling saw the king on the chess board falling over in defeat but she was too sleepy to know whose it was. Feargeal had won the first game she knew, but who had won the second?

She supposed she would find out at noon the next day when the fifty mares and cows and storytellers and chess players appeared on the road. But on they went to Emain Macha. Could it be possible that this plucky young warrior could have been a match for Emer?

When the three reached Emain Macha, Aoife gave birth to a daughter and everyone rejoiced. Emer and Aisling were with her in the stone circle. Emer had buried the afterbirth under an Ogham stone, it was already a full moon, and Deirdre, Aoife's daughter was sucking happily at her mother's breast.

A great feast was prepared to celebrate Emer's triumph over the evil prophecy and Emer and Feargeal were married. The whole company showered them with blessings and good wishes. Emer alone was downcast. She had broken her pledge not to wed any man living before Samhain and knew she would be dead by the morning.

The Red Branch Knights took to the fields, jousting, racing, leaping and performing a host of heroic feats. When Feargeal made the hero's salmon leap for the seventh time he landed on the point of his spear. A roar went up from the crowd who feared the worst but no blood was spilt, only his tunic was torn across the chest. A sigh of relief went round the assembly and then more shouts and pointing and heads bobbing, trying to see the cause of the uproar. Feargeal bowed to Emer who rose to her feet in astonishment. This was no knight standing before her, this was a woman.

She jumped to the ground and hugged Feargeal to her breast, weeping at the thought that she hadn't married a man at all and no early death awaited her. But the crowd's protests grew louder and Aoife approached the woman demanding an explanation. Before she had time to speak a man stormed through the crowd and took his place beside Emer.

'I am Feargeal,' he said simply, 'and this is my twin sister Findige. She was reared as a boy, taught all the feats of a warrior and she is equal to me in skill and prowess with weapons.'

'That is surely true,' said Aoife, 'as we all have witnessed.'

'Findige fought in this tournament to save my honour, for I was under a geasa not to wield my spear till the night of Samhain had passed.' At this Aoife was well pleased and welcomed Feargeal and Findige to the feast.

Everyone marvelled at the likeness between brother and sister. With her armour on, it was impossible to tell that Findige was a woman, and indeed impossible to tell one from the other. Except for a birth mark, a mole on Feargeal's thumb, they could be the same person. Which one did Emer marry, everyone wanted to know. No one knew for sure and the story of Emer's wedding day and all the events that went before was told and retold through the long nights of the winter.

Findige declared that she must return to her people.

'You have done well,' said Aoife, 'you are always welcome here.' Emer, Feargeal and Aisling prepared to return to Luachra. Aoife showered them with gifts and they had to take Emer's fifty grey mares as packhorses.

As they rounded the side of Cruachan the Fairy Hill, Feargeal removed his gauntlet. Aisling stared at his thumb, Emer smiled, and as the three women rode on to Luachra, Findige's mare let out a loud raucous sound, so that she seemed to be neighing with laughter.

Joni Crone

Än Irish Fairy Tale

ONCE upon a time, in the land of saints and scholars, there lived a handsome young man named Kevin. One day he decided to retreat from the world and spend the rest of his life giving praise to god as a holy hermit. He then went to live high upon a ledge in a wild remote place indeed, called Glendalough, in the county of Wicklow. Now, there was also, at the same time, in the land of saints and scholars, a beautiful maiden, whose name is forgotten on account of the fact that it was never considered worth remembering. Well, didn't this beautiful maiden fall madly in love with the holy hermit. She made lots of attempts to talk to him, to get him to come down off his lonely ledge, for she wanted him to fall in love with her too and come away down and marry her. He didn't want to at all so he did a lot of praying, meditating, and confabbing with god, and after he was finished he decided to put an end to her wooing — and he did. The next time she came up to him he shoved her down off the top of his high ledge and she got broke into smithereens on the rocks far down below, and god was very pleased with the holy hermit. When he died, many years later, as an old, old man, the people of Ireland acclaimed him as a saint. And ever since, droves of nuns, from all over Ireland, converge on his tomb, annually, every year, to pray for the great virtue of chastity as practised by holy Saint Kevin, the patron saint of woman beaters.

Frances Molloy

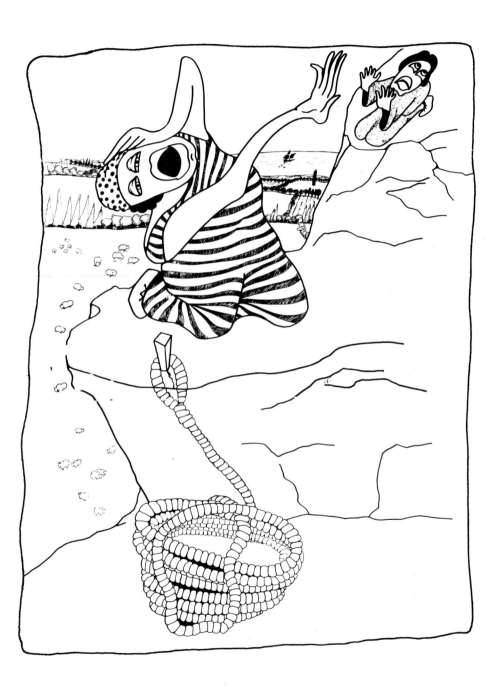

Dick Whittington and her Cat

FOR as long as she could remember Dick Whittington has wanted to go to London. Everyone knew this, especially her cat who by now was sick and tired of hearing her owner go on about it. 'Oh get on with it then,' she snapped irritably at Dick one day, 'and go to London before you drive me crazy talking about the place.' Dick was amazed on two counts — firstly, she was either going mental or she was the owner of the only talking cat she had ever come across. Secondly, she hadn't realised just how much she had annoyed her cat who, for lack of a better title, went under the name of *Moggy*. You will gather, dear reader, from the aforementioned that very little, in fact no thought at all was given to the cat's name who, as a result, felt extremely put out and forever afterwards displayed a less than equable temperament.

Anyway to get on with the story . . . Dick decided there and then she was going to London that very day. There was only one problem — she had no money to 'let the train take the strain,' and would have to hitchhike. But then, as she was about to set off, Dick met a friend of hers who was driving a minibus to London in order to collect some material for the local women's sewing co-op. Jemima dropped her off near the Tower of London, slipped a fiver into her denim jacket, and drove off wishing her the best of luck.

'Right then,' muttered Dick to herself, 'first things first, get myself fixed up in accommodation for the night and go lookin' for a job first thing tomorrow.'

Finding somewhere that took cats as well as people was not an easy task, but Dick was a resourceful woman and found herself a live-in job within hours. She had no intention of staying however, this was merely phase 1 of her plan. Phase 2 was to get a job in the Stock Exchange, learn about the business and eventually become a stockbroker.

Several months later Dick was on her way. She made herself invaluable as an Administrative Assistant to the managing director of the most reputable firm of stockbrokers in London, Goodbody, Goodbody & Goodbody. The last-mentioned of those Goodbody's was a bad lot, but we'll get back to that later.

One day Dick applied for a vacancy as a trainee stockbroker. She surprised her boss a little but when he had time to think about it he realised that it would have many advantages for him, not least being that here was someone whom he could really trust.

Time passed and Dick became proficient in dealing — the jargon of the trade — bulls, bears, venture capital and equities and gilts were no longer a mystery to her. In fact she was so good that she was acknowledged by all and sundry as the best and most honest stockbroker in the city.

Phase 3 of her plan was to set up her own firm — which she duly did and trained many women in the not-so-gentle art of stockbroking. She considered women to be more honest, more reliable and less lazy than their male counterparts. Her firm gradually became synonymous with honesty and reliability, while making a very good profit.

Not every firm in the city was whiter than white in the honesty stakes and the term 'insider dealing' was bandied about a lot, particularly in reference to the third Goodbody — the black sheep of the family so to speak. Sly Goodbody was suspected of fraud, but this had not yet been proved.

Dick Whittington was commissioned by the Chairperson of the Stock Exchange to investigate the third Goodbody's murky activities. This she accomplished by getting one of her own staff to apply for a job vacancy and report back regularly to her. Soon she had enough evidence to prove her case and Sly Goodbody was dealt with by the Chairperson and duly convicted. His future in stockbroking was none too rosy when the word got out that he had been caught napping. His crime

was perceived by many as being caught rather than the illegal practice of dealing in shares of a company on the verge of a takeover.

Dick's integrity did not go unnoticed, and she was duly honoured by being elected to the City Council and then finally as Mayor of London. This was Phase 4 and the final one of her plan.

All had been achieved and in her post as Mayor she strategically placed women in decision making roles; she channelled funds into community groups, such as women's groups, children's playgroups, literacy schemes and adult education. In the years that followed she changed the accepted order of things, inspiring similar revolution around the world, thus ensuring that the vulnerable members of society were catered for, as should be the case in all civilised society.

Anne Killeen

'A funny, sassy, heretical collection of feminist fairytales'

MS MUFFET AND OTHERS
Fairy Tales for Feminists

Ms Muffet and Others is the second in our collection of fairy tales for feminists. The first, *Rapunzel's Revenge*, was highly acclaimed for its originality and style.

Told from a feminist perspective, *Ms Muffet and Others* is a unique collection of fairy tales and fables. Each writer presents, what was the traditional, in an unorthodox and challenging way. The nine contributors, including Maeve Kelly, Leland Bardwell, Liz McManus, Evelyn Conlon and Máirín Johnston, cover a broad spectrum of literary talent, moving from the straight, or even crooked humour of *The Woodcutter's Daughter*, to the sensitive and evocative language of *The Selkie*.

The critics were unreserved in their praise for *Rapunzel's Revenge*, and will, without doubt, receive *Ms Muffet and Others* with the same enthusiasm.

'*Rapunzel's Revenge*, a funny, sassy, heretical collection of fairy tales.'   *Irish Times.*

ISBN 0 946211 272 £3.50 $6.50 pb   Illustrated
64pp. Size: 6" × 8¼"

RAPUNZEL'S REVENGE
Fairy Tales for Feminists

'Rapunzel's Revenge is a feminist re-writing of fairy tales which has Mary Maher revealing that Snow White organised the seven dwarfs into a trade union, Maeve Binchy exposing Cinderella's prince as a foot fetishist, and a truly gifted Joni Crone showing that feminist fairy tales can be written in fairy tale language. Wendy Shea's cartoon of Little Ms Muffet, saying to the spider 'C'mon, baby, frighten me to death' should be framed'.

In Dublin.

'Things will never be the same again down in the woods ... Maeve Binchy, Carolyn Swift, Mary Maher and several others give a sardonic feminist twist to the fairy tales we all grew up on.

Sunday Independent.

'Rapunzel's Revenge, a funny, sassy, heretical collection of fairytales...'

Irish Times.

ISBN 0 946211 18 3 £3.50 $6.50 pb   Illustrated
64pp. Size: 6″ × 8¼″

MORE MISSING PIECES (2)
Her Story of Irish Women

'. . . resurrects more forgotten Irish women like the sorceress who indicted a bishop for defamation of character; the medical student threatened with excommunication should she continue her studies; the Cork woman who was a pirate; and the hang woman of the Assizes, among others.'

Nell McCafferty, *In Dublin.*

More Missing Pieces is a colourful patchwork of over sixty Irish women's lives, adventures and exploits. It is a book with a difference.

ISBN 0 946211 17 5 £2.95 $5.95 pb   Illustrated
64pp. Size: 6" × 8¼"

DID YOUR GRANNY HAVE A HAMMER???
A History of the Irish Women's Suffrage Movement 1876-1922
Rosemary Cullen Owens (ed)

'A cheeky challenging title for a history of the Irish Suffrage Movement from 1876-1922. It is not a book like any other to me that seeks to write women back into history. It is meant to whet your appetite and encourage you to ask about your granny, and wake you up with a wink, a laugh and a nudge to the fact that women were up and about and doing, way back then.'

In Dublin.

This wide ranging and informative pack consists of 26 items, entertainingly presented and fully illustrated. An unusual feature of this pack is a facsimile of the *Irish Citizen* — an eight page special edition which includes leading articles taken throughout the paper's existence from 1912 to 1920.

ISBN 0 946211 14 0 £3.95 $6.95 pack   Illustrated

AROUND THE BANKS OF PIMLICO
Máirín Johnston

Around the Banks of Pimlico is a fascinating and delightful account of life in the Dublin Liberties over a period of a hundred years 1850-1950. It is a tribute to the people who lived, laughed, worked and suffered in one of Dublin's most colourful and celebrated streets.

After the famine in 1945, Máirín Johnston's great great grandmother moved to Pimlico from Gort, Co Tipperary, and four generations later the author compares what Pimlico was like then with what it was when her mother left it a generation later.

'... her volume lives up to the claim of being "a social history with a difference, written by a woman with a first hand knowledge and profound feeling for her subject" ... there's loads of life, times, history, customs, cures and characters in *Around the Banks of Pimlico'*.   *Irish Press.*

Around the Banks of Pimlico is beautifully illustrated with photographs, many previously unpublished, and drawings.

ISBN 0 946211 15 9 £5.95 £9.95 pb   ISBN 0 946211 16 7 £12.95 $24.95 hb Illustrated
144pp. Size: 6¾" × 9½"

SMASHING TIMES
A History of the Irish Women's Suffrage Movement
Rosemary Cullen Owens

'This is a book which urgently needs to be read by anyone interested in the foundation of modern Irish Society.'
Lucille Redmond, *Sunday Press.*

'A most enjoyable and worthwhile book both for the historian and general interested reader.'
Mary Leyden, *Roscommon Champion.*

Smashing Times brings to life the women of the nineteen hundreds who were active and militant suffragettes. It is a remarkable and rewarding account of the Irish Women's Franchise League who fought for women's right to vote.

ISBN 0 946211 08 6 £4.95 $8.50 pb   ISBN 0 946211 07 8 £10.00 $19.95 hb Illustrated
160pp. Size: 5" × 7½"